Act One

Gabriel Lilas stood over the stove, the aroma of dinner filling the kitchen as he prepared a meal for his wife, Colleen. At 28 years old, Gabriel possessed a striking appearance with his unique light purplish-blue hair and silver eyes. Tall and slender, he worked diligently at Takker Medical Center, crafting vaccines for children while Colleen labored on adult vaccines in the same facility.

Placing Colleen's plate on the table, Gabriel leaned in for a tender kiss.

Colleen: "How was work today, honey?"

Gabriel's expression darkened. "Sad. We ran out of vaccines, and 12 children succumbed in Iberaa. It weighs heavily on my mind."

Colleen's voice softened. "The shortage of Gray Willy's flowers for the vaccine isn't your fault, Gabe. This war is draining our resources."

Gabriel nodded, a shadow of concern in his eyes. "They stripped Thomas of his citizenship today. He's just sixteen."

Colleen's horror was palpable. "For what?!"

Gabriel's tone was grave. "For speaking out against the war. Be cautious, Colleen."

Colleen's resolve hardened. "I'm not naïve. I won't speak out in public. But Kara... she must be devastated about Thomas. I'll give her a call."

Gabriel's next words struck like a hammer. "Don't bother. She tried to help him, and now she's gone."

Colleen's gasp was one of disbelief. "Jesus!"

Gabriel's gaze was steady. "Yes, it's tragic. But we must tread carefully, or we'll meet the same fate."

Colleen's frustration boiled over. "I hate this country."

Gabriel's voice was tinged with sorrow. "There was a time when I loved it."

Colleen hesitated before revealing her burden. "I need to tell you something."

Gabriel took her hand, his concern evident. "What is it?"

Colleen's breath caught in her throat. "People have been dropping dead, and we suspect it's related to orange fever. The DNA... it's changing inexplicably, worsening illnesses."

Gabriel's stress was palpable as he absorbed the news. He blew out a breath and rubbed his face, seeking solace in his wife's embrace.

Colleen's voice was resolute. "We're working tirelessly to find answers."

The symptoms of orange fever echoed in their minds as they braced for the challenges ahead.

The following day, Gabriel's older brother, Reese, arrived to drive him to work. Gabriel, plagued by a fear of driving, relied on Reese's support. As they approached the Iberaa Border, tension mounted as police officers scrutinized their papers.

Reese handed over Gabriel's documents, and the officer's attention was drawn to Gabriel's unconventional appearance.

Officer 1: "Whoa, your hair!"

Gabriel quipped with a smile, "Just born this way. Cool, right?"

Laughter filled the air as they passed through, Reese's arm around Gabriel in a show of solidarity.

At Takker, Reese broached a sensitive topic with his brother, offering to teach him to drive. Despite his fears, Gabriel found solace in the idea of bonding with Reese and the prospect of teaching his future children to drive.

As Gabriel entered his workplace, the weight of the world bore down on him, the conflict between Spinlenian and Ash-Lork territories looming large in his mind."

Gabriel's friend, Jotmad, taps him on the shoulder, and Gabriel turns to greet him, only to be met with a whispered revelation.

Jotmad: "They're bringing back the draft."

A wave of fear washes over Gabriel as he feels a chill run down his spine. Fumbling for his phone, he texts a friend, expressing his concern about being drafted. Jotmad reassures him that government workers like themselves are safe from conscription.

With a sigh of relief, Gabriel tucks his phone away and heads to his designated work area. As he navigates the halls of Section AQ, transporting vaccines to where they are needed, he encounters his wife, Colleen. A quick exchange of gestures and a high-five pass between them as they go about their respective duties.

Donning protective gear, Gabriel enters the sick ward, attending to children in need before tending to the necessary paperwork. Thirty minutes later, he's free to leave for the day. Colleen surprises him with a hug as he clocks out.

Colleen: "I wish I could come with you."

Gabriel offers words of reassurance. "We'll be together again soon, just three hours away."

Colleen's frustration is palpable. "I can't stand it."

After a tender moment, Gabriel offers her his lunch, noticing their tight budget.

Gabriel: "I won't be needing this. You can have it since we're low on food."

Despite her half-hearted smile, Colleen remains determined.

Colleen: "We're fine. I'll get groceries when I receive my bonus on Tuesday."

Gabriel expresses his longing for support from friends, but Colleen brushes it off, citing their financial struggles. As they part ways, Gabriel promises to discuss something happier when they get home.

As Gabriel heads out with his brother, Reese, the looming threat of the draft weighs heavily on their minds. Reese expresses his fears of being conscripted and contemplates fleeing to Lundy. Gabriel cautions against such actions, knowing the consequences. However, Gabriel's own health becomes a concern as Reese notices his brother's pallor and discomfort.

Reese's touch on Gabriel's feverish face highlights the gravity of their situation.

Reese: You feel like you're burning up. Did you eat something bad?

Gabriel: (Shaking his head) Not a bite. I was just about to head home, anyway. Colleen will be back soon.

Reese: You sure you don't want a ride?

Gabriel: Thanks, but I think I'll walk. Clear my head.

He offers a weak smile, then pushes off, his gait slightly unsteady. Reese watches him go, a worried frown replacing her concern.

INT. THE LILACS HOME - DAY

Gabriel unlocks the door and finds Colleen in the living room, a medical textbook open on her lap. He stumbles towards the couch, collapsing beside her.

Colleen: Gabe! What's wrong?

Gabriel: (Groaning) Not sure. Feel...weird.

Colleen: (Concerned) We're doctors, honey. Any ideas?

Gabriel: Maybe a bug? Haven't eaten anything yet.

Colleen: Leftovers are in the fridge. I'll heat them up.

Moments later

Colleen places a steaming plate in front of Gabriel. He takes a tentative bite, then another, color slowly returning to his cheeks.

Colleen: Feeling better?

Gabriel: Much. Maybe it was just hunger pains.

Colleen: (Smiling) So, what did you want to talk about?

Gabriel: (Taking a deep breath) I... I want a kid.

Colleen's eyes widen in surprise, then melt into pure joy.

Colleen: (Voice thick with emotion) Really?

Gabriel: Don't you?

Colleen leans in, her answer a tender kiss that speaks volumes.

Act Two:

Gabriel receives a somber visit from two Spinlenian soldiers, bearing news that shakes him to the core. The impending threat of Ash soldiers and lurking spies forces a swift evacuation by Friday, May 29th. Hastily, Takker workers, including Gabriel and his family, gather their essentials - vaccines, documents, and weapons - preparing to flee the city.

As they journey to a hotel in the northern part of their country, Gabriel's mind is plagued by discomfort. A headache gnaws at him, intensifying as thoughts of Colleen flood his mind. Despite his physical discomfort, Gabriel finds himself unable to shake the sense of foreboding that looms over them all.

Arriving at the hotel, Gabriel seeks solace in a shower, but his headache persists, adding to his growing unease. Meanwhile, tensions between Gabriel and Colleen escalate as they confront the grim reality of their situation. Colleen's desire to abandon Spinlenia clashes with

Gabriel's sense of duty and attachment to their homeland.

Amidst their heated exchange, Gabriel conceals his worsening condition from Colleen, swallowing his own pain to alleviate hers. However, as night falls, Gabriel's health takes a turn for the worse. Stomach pains and vomiting wrack his body, prompting concern from his brother, Reese.

Gabriel's physical deterioration becomes apparent, his eyes sunken and weary. Despite Reese's offer to accompany him to the doctor, Gabriel insists on shielding Colleen from further worry, choosing instead to suffer in silence. But as he grapples with his deteriorating health, Gabriel's chance encounter with an old high-school friend, Liza Dehultz, at the registration office, adds another layer of complexity to his already tumultuous journey.

Liza: Gabriel Lilas!? Long time no see! What brings you here, my fellow countryman?

Gabriel, his discomfort evident, tries to hide his unease as he coughs into a handkerchief. He's spits orange and black gunk.

Liza's concern deepens as she notices his condition. Gabriel clears his throat before responding.

Gabriel: It's good to see you too. How is Robbie?

Liza: We got married, seven kids, and three dogs. It’s a good life, just hoping those asshats surrender soon.

Gabriel: Yeah.

Liza: Are you okay? You look like hell.

Gabriel: Yeah, I'll be fine. I got married too, you know.

Liza: Really? To whom?

Gabriel: Her name is Colleen. I met her in medical school. She's a blessing, but no kids yet, though we're trying.

Liza: Just... make sure to have fun every night. I've got seven, so what brings you here?

Gabriel discreetly kicks the camera under Liza's desk, catching her attention.

Gabriel: We've got about 13 minutes before they realize it's not them.

Liza: What do you need, Gabe?

Gabriel: Reese cannot go to work can do mark down he is disable.

Liza hesitates, aware of the risks involved.

Gabriel: Do it now, then pass it through the random system. They won't know who reported it.

Liza: You're still the same old nerd. Alright, I'll do it.

Reluctantly, Liza complies, filling out the report on Reese. Gabriel places money on the table, but Liza refuses, insisting it's a favor between friends.

Later, at a dinner party thrown by Colleen to celebrate her bonus, Gabriel feels increasingly exhausted. After a brief conversation with friends, Emily notices something alarming -

blood staining Gabriel's pants. Before anyone can react, Gabriel convulses violently, vomiting blood and losing consciousness.

Emergency services are called, and Gabriel is rushed to the hospital, where he falls into a coma.

Act Three:

Colleen receives overwhelming support from friends and family at the hospital. Emily, her 15-year-old son Cellrod, and Reese are by Gabriel's bedside when Dr. Moci Lovely enters the room.

Dr. Lovely: He has orange fever.

Colleen collapses in tears, but Gabriel suddenly blinks awake, alarming everyone in the room.

Cellrod: He’s awake!

The doctor rushes to Gabriel's side, conducting tests as Colleen and the others watch anxiously.

Dr. Lovely: Mr. Lilas, can you speak?

But Gabriel remains silent, only blinking in response. The doctor examines his DNA, revealing an ominous orange line.

Dr. Lovely: This shouldn't be here. The fever is forming in the middle of his DNA. It's severe, I'm afraid. Terminal.

Colleen's face contorts with fear as Emily comforts her.

Reese: How long does he have?

Dr. Lovely studies Gabriel's DNA again, her expression grave.

Dr. Lovely: He could go any day now.

Colleen's cry fills the room as the doctor exits, leaving the family to confront the grim reality ahead.

Reese: Why don’t you go get some fresh air, Celly?

Cellrod: I want to be here for Gabe and Colleen.

Reese: You're a sweet boy, but I can see it's weighing on you, son.

Cellrod: I never knew my dad, and Gabe was like a father to me. He invited Mom and me over for all the holidays. He never left me in my time of need, so I can't leave him.

Emily: Honey, you know if you get too stressed out, you get very sick. Go get some fresh air.

Cellrod: What if he dies while I'm away?

Colleen: He's pretty much gone now. Take care of yourself, Celly. Gabe would have wanted that.

Cellrod stands and walks out of the room. Colleen plays with Gabriel's bluish-purple hair and kisses his lips.

Colleen looks into Gabriel's lifeless eyes and closes hers as tears trickle down, crashing onto Gabriel's face.

Emily: Everything will be okay, buddy.

Colleen scoffs and lays her head on Gabriel's chest, hearing his weak heartbeat.

Colleen: No, it won't.

A Week Later

Colleen drives recklessly to the hospital after hearing that Gabriel is awake and talking. She crashes her car into a tree, hops out, and runs to his room. Once there, their eyes meet at the door.

Colleen: Gabe!

Gabriel: My sweet Colleen!

Colleen rushes over to her husband and kisses his hand and face.

Colleen has tears in her eyes.

Colleen: How are you, love?

Gabriel closes his eyes, shielding them from the light, and lays down shirtless.

Gabriel: Lights hurt me, so keep them out.

Colleen: Of course, honey.

Gabriel begins to get emotional.

Gabriel: I might die any day, huh?

Colleen: Maybe you won't, you're speaking.

Gabriel: My bones feel like water. I feel like death. I'm not getting better, babe.

Colleen: I'm so close to a cure. I've been working around the clock, off the clock. I'm so close, Gabe.

Gabriel: Let me go.

Colleen is hurt, and she screams in his direction as tears of blood run down his face.

Gabriel: I'm going to die, my love. Prepare for it, prepare for it now.

Colleen: Gabe, I'm pregnant!

Gabriel drops his head in shock.

Gabriel: I'm lost for words... But I am happy.

Colleen: I'm so close, honey. You will get to know him or her.

Gabriel slams his fist on the table next to her, a rare display of anger, his eyes surrounded by dark rings.

Gabriel: As your husband, you will obey me. You need to give up this false hope of a cure because it’s killing me, and I'm so damn tired. You need to prepare for my passing and be strong, for our child. You need to accept that there is no cure, Colleen Lilas.

Colleen, her hand resting on her belly, weeps silently.

Gabriel: I'm going to write them a letter. You'll give it to them when they are 16.

Gabriel grabs a piece of paper and a pencil and begins to write the letter.

Colleen: Sure.

Act Four

Colleen is deeply engrossed in her research, neglecting everything else. Emily joins her, noticing Colleen's disheveled appearance - her hair messy, the smell of sweat clinging to her, and wearing the same clothes for three days.

Emily: How's everything going?

Colleen doesn't respond, focusing on testing different cures on the infected DNA.

Emily: I think I found a solution to your issue.

Colleen: How?

She replies, not looking up.

Emily: A lady named Lisa Wu will stop by the hospital today to explain. She can help.

Colleen looks up at her friend with a blank stare.

Colleen: Okay.

On the way to the hospital, Colleen sits silently in the backseat as Reese drives.

Reese: Colleen, when he dies, I want you to move in with me.

Colleen scowls.

Reese: He's going to die of yellow fever.

Colleen: I KNOW WHAT HE IS!!

Reese: Don't yell, it's harsh on the child inside you, darling. I want you to move in with me.

Colleen: Why?

Reese: That's my niece or nephew. They need to have a strong man in their life, a father figure. I want to be that for them. And, no offense, but you know how Cellrod is. He is fatherless.

Colleen: Celly is a good kid.

Reese: He’s fatherless, and you know he acts out. Remember when he broke that kid’s arm with that bat?

Colleen: What do you expect? He just wants to know his father.

Reese: And I don't want my little niece or nephew to go through that. So, what do you say, move in with me?

Colleen: Do you know why I can't? Gabriel is the love of my life. I'm not ready to lose him.

Reese: Life is not fair, dear.

When Reese and Colleen reach Gabriel's room, he's resting as Lisa Wu looks down at him.

Reese: Do you know my brother, Miss?

Lisa turns to face them.

Lisa: I’m Lisa Wu, a government scientist. I am here to talk to Colleen Lilas.

Colleen: Did Emily Fendrick send you?

Lisa nods.

Lisa: Let's go for a walk.

As the two women walk, Lisa breaks the silence.

Lisa: He has orange fever, huh?

Colleen nods.

Lisa: I have an offer for you, Colleen.

Colleen: What's the offer?

Lisa: I work with Torjork. We've been dabbling with cloning human beings, and we were successful with a few. We can clone your husband. It will be a copy of him.

Colleen: A copy with the fever?

Colleen snickers at Lisa.

Lisa: We cloned a woman with the fever; her clone did not have it.

Colleen ponders the thought, but she knows nothing comes for free.

Colleen: What does the government want?

Lisa grins.

Lisa: Smart question. You let us use him for the war. We need more men. We'll use Gabriel for six years, then return him to you.

Colleen: He will never survive, or he's a pawn.

Lisa: If you agree to the cloning, we will scan a copy of all his memories and consciousness. Don't worry; when he wakes, he will still be himself. When we clone him, he will still be himself. They start blank, so we have to copy their memories, and that level of empathy is what makes them themselves again.

Colleen looks worried and confused.

Lisa: Or you can go through with his death.

Colleen: Reese will not be cool with this.

Lisa: He is your husband, Colleen.

Colleen: I don’t even think Gabriel will be cool with this.

Lisa frowns and places her hands on Colleen.

Lisa: Emily said you are pregnant. Don't you want Gabriel? Think about that baby.

Colleen begins to weep.

Colleen: Okay, okay, I’ll do it.

Colleen asks Reese to go for a walk with her so Lisa can copy Gabriel's memories and consciousness. She places a device on the back of his head, scanning his memories. Gabriel opens his eyes and looks up at her.

Gabriel: What are you doing to me?

Lisa: Saving you from death. Goodbye, Gabriel.

Gabriel then passes out from exhaustion caused by the chip copying his memories.

Later that day, Gabriel opens his eyes to see his brother Reese sleeping in a chair as his wife leans in, grabbing his hand.

Gabriel: Everything hurts... that woman was here. (Colleen sits on the bed) She said she was saving me from death.

Colleen: That was Lisa. She's from the government.

Gabriel: Oh? Why was she here?

Colleen: It's a long story, but she told me that when you died, she could clone you. It would be a copy of you.

Gabriel looks drained, turning away from her, his expression confused.

Gabriel: I'd be healed.

Colleen: Not exactly. She'd have your consciousness, and she'd have to plug that into your clone.

Gabriel: So, I'll be dead, but there will be a clone of me, and the clone will be blank. But there's a chip with my memories on it?

Colleen: Yes.

Gabriel: Why are they helping low citizens like us?

Colleen: I must sign you over to the war for six years.

Gabriel laughs.

Gabriel: So, they hold my consciousness, so I can be a blank killing machine, huh?

Colleen nods.

Gabriel: No.

Colleen: No, what?

Gabriel: No, they cannot copy me.

Colleen: Don't you want to be around for our kids? A child needs a father around; they're troubled without one.

Gabriel looks toward the doorway, where they see Emily and Cellrod. Cellrod storms out, and Emily follows.

Colleen, ashamed, covers her mouth, feeling embarrassed for what she said.

Colleen: Oh, fuck.

Gabriel: Marry Reese.

Colleen: What? No! I don't like him like that, you know that!

Gabriel: It’s best for our ba……

The machines start beeping and buzzing, waking Reese up. He runs over to Gabriel, who is not moving.

Reese shakes him as Colleen runs to get a doctor.

Gabriel Marsal Lilas

Dies on Saturday afternoon at

Toramlor Hospital

Colleen identifies Gabriel, then calls Lisa. She arrives within 15 minutes. Colleen was so upset she wouldn’t leave Gabriel's side. She was crying, on the verge of a nervous breakdown.

Lisa: Is it okay if I go in and get some DNA from your husband?

Colleen, with her hands over her face, does give her permission.

Lisa walks into the room, pulls back the sheet, and sees a pillow beside Gabriel. She takes out a knife from her bag, cuts off a finger from him, and puts it in her bag.

Lisa hugs Colleen.

Lisa: Don’t have a funeral for him. Wait.

Act Five

"Wake up, Gabriel!"

He does. He opens his silver eyes and takes a breath, many breaths.

"Stop! Relax. Sit up."

The man, the clone of Gabriel, sits up and stands. He is in an all-white room and bolts for the door with no windows.

"Stop! Relax, Clone!"

Clone: "Where am I?"

"You are in a government base. Today is your birthday, you skinbutt. It’s May 26th. Happy birthday."

Clone: "Who am I?"

"You are a clone of Gabriel Lilas, so you are Gabriel Lilas."

Gabriel: "I don't remember anything."

"You are a clone, only a few days old. You are 28 years old, and you have a pregnant wife, an older brother, and deceased parents."

Gabriel: "Why did you clone Gabriel?"

"He died."

Gabriel: "Oh."

"On day 20, you will undergo war training. You will kill as many Ash men as you can. After 6

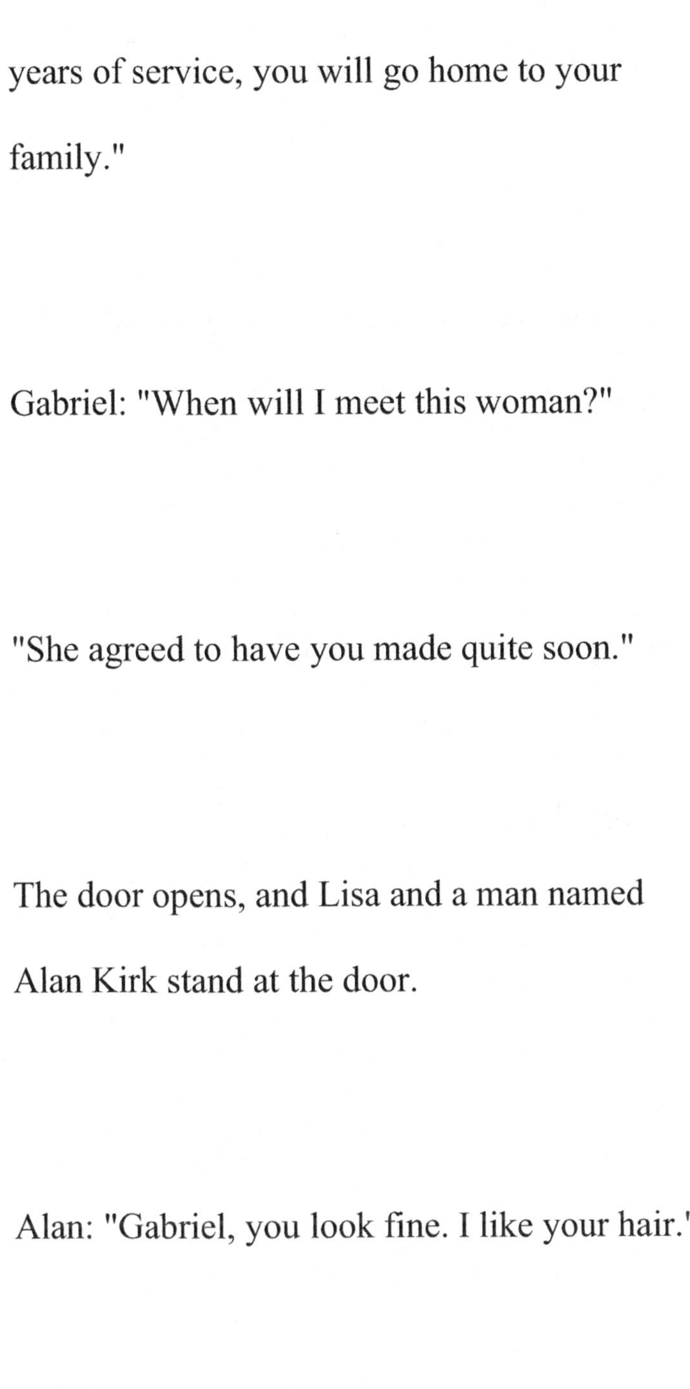

years of service, you will go home to your family."

Gabriel: "When will I meet this woman?"

"She agreed to have you made quite soon."

The door opens, and Lisa and a man named Alan Kirk stand at the door.

Alan: "Gabriel, you look fine. I like your hair."

Gabriel: "What's wrong with it?"

Lisa: "Nothing, it's purplish-blue, your natural hair color. Now, let’s feed you."

Gabriel eats for 3 hours straight. This was typical for clones when they woke up; they were very hungry.

The Graveyard

Colleen looks at Gabriel's headstone and wraps her arms around it, crying. She remembers their first kiss in college and their first date at the state fair when they were 21. She recalls a memory of moving into her dorm, feeling nervous, and Gabriel helping her. It's a beautiful memory that comforts her during this lonely day.

But now, she has a new visitor. Colleen sets a table, nervous to meet the clone of her husband. A beep goes off, and soldiers open the door. Then, the clone of Gabriel walks in. He looks just like him, and he strides over to the table where she is. She fights back tears as they fall down her face.

Gabriel places his hand in his lap and gives her a warm smile.

Gabriel: "I am sorry for your loss."

He frowns.

Colleen: "It's all right, Gabriel. You exist. Did they tell you who I am?"

Gabriel: "My wife. They told me everything."

Gabriel clears his throat.

Colleen wipes her eyes.

Colleen: "I love you!"

Gabriel leans in. Gabriel: Do you know when they will give me my memories?

She clears her throat.

Gabriel: I want to remember you so I can say it back to you.

Colleen: I'm not sure. Are you scared about war?

Gabriel cocks his head to one side, a bit confused.

Gabriel: I'm very strong. I broke a cinder block with my hands yesterday. No, I am not, but maybe I should be. I saw what happened when men died on the telly.

Colleen: You will be alright, okay? You've got my love and your child’s love.

She takes Gabriel by his hair, pulls his head to her belly, and places his head onto her belly so he can hear the baby moving around. He smiles so big and giggles.

Gabriel: Do you want a boy or girl?

Colleen: Anything healthy. What about you?

Gabriel: Anything healthy.

That night at Reese's house, Colleen sips a glass of whiskey, looking at the photos she took with the clone of Gabe. Reese stands behind her with a smile, holding a beer.

Reese: Our friends asked me to check on you.

Colleen: I'll be back in soon, just a moment.

Reese: I know you miss him.

Colleen comes around to face Reese.

Colleen: I have to tell you something.

Reese: What do you have to tell me?

Colleen puts her hands on his face, smiling and giggling.

Colleen: I let them clone Gabe !”

Reese is quiet for a moment, then starts drinking his beer.

Colleen: You're not saying anything.

Reese: That’s a mean joke. My little brother's dead.

Colleen shows Reese the picture of her and the clone of Gabriel in a medical room. It had today’s date on it. Reese just stares at it for a long moment.

Reese: This is my brother on today’s date. He looks happy, wearing his same clothes.

Colleen: I was going to throw them out, but he's healthy and happy.

Reese: Take me to him now!

Colleen: He doesn't remember us.

Reese: If he's an exact clone, how can he not?

Colleen: In order to clone him, I had to sign him over to the war for 6 years. And he’s not an exact clone. They had to take a chip of his memory. But in order for him to get the memories, he has to do service first.

Reese is blown away. He is angry.

Reese: What? He can't handle that, Gabe's? Why would you do that?

Colleen: Because I will never want to see him again, Reese. They had me by the horns.

Reese: You just wanted to see him again. I want to see him.

Visit Two

Reese steps into the room where Gabriel is being held. Reese grabs him from behind, kisses the back of his neck, and lets go. Gabriel turns to face him as Colleen walks through the door. Gabriel smiles big at him, looking past Reese. Lisa is in the doorway with a clipboard, taking notes.

Lisa: Gabriel, this man is your brother. Don't be rude.

Gabriel focuses on Reese’s green eyes, crying, holding back his emotions. Gabriel embraces him as his wife comes over.

Reese: Brother!

Gabriel and Reese let go of each other, then he pulls him back in.

Gabriel: I'm sorry my death was rough on you. What is your name, brother?

Reese: Reese Lilas. I am your big brother.

Gabriel: Awesome. (Looks over at Colleen) You couldnt have stayed away, couldn’t you?

She giggles and grabs Gabriel's chin, kissing him.

Reese: So, you're going to war?

Gabriel: I start basic training in the morning, in the south.

Colleen and Reese both look over at Lisa with shock.

Colleen: You didn't tell me he was starting so soon.

Lisa: He’s needed, so we will ship him out soon.

Reese: So, we can't see him anymore?

Lisa: Weekends, he'll be at Camp Trevor. You can see him in the south.

Colleen strokes Gabriel's face with a smile and tells him everything will be okay, even though she knew that it probably wouldn’t be.

Reese: What if he gets killed?

Colleen: Reese!?

Lisa: This is not the end of the world; we’ll just clone him again.

Gabriel props his feet on the table, carefree.

Gabriel: Don't worry, guys. I'll be extra careful.

Colleen: My sweet Gabriel, of course you will.

Reese: I have $10,000 in my bank. Let us walk out with him and his memories.

Lisa laughs.

Lisa: That wasn't the deal.

Reese: Please, take every penny I have. I just want my brother.

Colleen: Reese! Stop it!

Reese: Shut up, Colleen!

Gabriel: Be gentle; it may not even be 6 years.

Lisa: Very wise, Gabriel! He is right. I know you miss him, but we had an agreement. I'm sorry.

Lisa steps out of the room, and Reese punches a wall.

Reese: Fuck!

Reese falls to his knees and weeps, and Gabriel sits next to him.

Reese: When you were little, our parents used to make us work on the farm. They exhausted you so much. You weren't a farm boy; you were more of an education type. You had your head in books and such. You always did your work so you could rest. I saw how smart you were with books; farmwork was not for you. It was education. That was for you.

Gabriel drops his head.

Gabriel: I wish I could remember.

Reese: They're whores for not letting you.

Colleen is touched by watching Gabriel and Reese bond. In the car ride back home, they ride in silence for a while, then Reese breaks the ice.

Reese: Something is fishy about Lisa and her company.

Colleen: Why? Because she wouldn't give you Gabe?

Reese: No, because she won't give him his memories. They're holding it as a pawn, but I don't know why. And him going to basic so soon, and she said not a word to you about it.

Colleen: She's busy, I'm sure she was going to, but you can't freak out like that. They could think something and cut us off from him.

Reese: It looked just like him.

Colleen: Gabriel is back; he will be with us again.

The next day, Cellrod knocks on Colleen's door in the morning. He tells her that he is feeling suicidal because he does not have a father in his life. Colleen tells Cellrod that he needs to talk to his mother about the situation. He says that he went through her things and found out who his father was, that she had an affair with a one of her college friends.

Act Six

Colleen's voice trembled as Emily confirmed the affair. The image of her son, threatening to take his own life, flickered in Colleen's mind. "He can't talk to his father," Emily insisted, her voice tight. "He just...can't." The weight of the situation pressed down on Colleen. Ignoring the judgment in Emily's eyes, she focused on getting help for her son.

On the Bus

Forty-five pairs of eyes scrutinized Gabriel on the crowded bus. All except John Hatchet, a nineteen-year-old with a mop of blonde curls, who offered a tentative smile. John whispered, "Clone?"

Gabriel, his voice barely above a croak, confirmed it. "How'd you know?"

"Word travels fast," John said, his youthful face etched with a somberness that belied his years. "They said you died. Orange fever?"

A pang of grief echoed in Gabriel for his lost loved ones. "Yeah," he muttered.

Suddenly, Patrick Cojeds, a hulking figure, loomed over them. "So, you're a damn skincopy, huh?"

Gabriel straightened, but his voice faltered, "I'm Gabriel Lilas."

Patrick scoffed. "Dead Gabriel Lilas. You ain't no soldier, no real man. Just cargo." A chorus of laughter erupted as Patrick swaggered away.

John placed a comforting hand on Gabriel's shoulder. "Don't mind him. He hates skincopies. We're on the same team, you and me."

"Countrymen," Gabriel corrected, a flicker of defiance igniting within him.

Baptism by Blood

The following hours were a brutal baptism by fire. Gabriel, more adept with firearms than hand-to-hand combat, found himself battered and bruised. Exhausted, he showered, the water washing away not just grime, but a sliver of his innocence. Another grueling three hours of water training barely left him the energy to stand.

At 4:00 AM, a jarring wake-up call jolted Gabriel from sleep. In the courtyard, a man, Tome GoHutz, stood tied to a pole, his face a canvas of pain. A single, vacant eye stared accusingly. General Alec Walsec, his voice dripping with malice, pronounced Tome a traitor for attempting escape. He then cast his gaze upon Gabriel, the only soldier not making eye contact.

"Gabriel Lilas," he boomed, pulling Gabriel's dog tags down. "Let's see what took you the first time."

Gabriel, his voice barely a whisper, revealed the cause of his demise: orange fever.

The general chuckled, a cruel sound. "A shame. But you'll do. You see this coward?" He gestured towards Tome. "We need volunteers to make an example."

Panic clawed at Gabriel's throat as the general's eyes narrowed. He knew he was the target. A cold metal object pressed into his clammy palm – a knife.

The Choice

"You'll kill someday, boy," the general sneered. "This can be your first."

Gabriel's entire being rebelled. He couldn't take a life, not like this. Yet, the general's chilling threat of another cloning echoed in his mind. With a heavy heart, he approached Tome.

"I'm sorry," Gabriel rasped, his voice thick with despair.

Tome, his defiance unwavering, spat back, "Die trying, boy. Don't be sorry for me. I'm free."

With a choked sob, Gabriel plunged the knife forward. A scream ripped through the air, followed by an unsettling silence.

The Call

Back in his dorm, Gabriel dialed his wife's number at the ungodly hour of 4:23 AM. Sleepily, Colleen answered.

"Colleen?" Gabriel's voice cracked. Tears welled up, blurring his vision.

"Gabe? What's wrong?" Her voice sharpened with concern.

"They...they made me kill someone," he choked out.

Colleen lurched upright in bed, a gasp escaping her lips. "A soldier?"

"He tried to escape," Gabriel explained between sobs. "They made me end him."

The horror in his voice sent shivers down Colleen's spine. "Oh, God, Gabriel," she whispered, her heart breaking for him.

"I can't stay here," he pleaded. "This place is evil."

Before he could finish, the door burst open. Three soldiers – Patrick, Gul, and Sede – stormed in, their faces contorted with malicious glee.

They jump Gabriel.

Emily carefully placed some of the roses in her bag and shot Colleen an irritated look.

Colleen: What's wrong?

Emily: He's a doctor, and he's married, his dad is. We had a one-night stand. Cellrod wasn't...

His wife is sick with cancer. This will destroy her.

Colleen: Why were you with a married man?

Emily covered her eyes, trying to hide her tears.

Emily: I was young! He was handsome. I thought I was in love. And now Celly will face rejection.

Colleen: How can you be so sure?

Emily: He's not meeting him! End of story.

Colleen: He said he'd kill himself if he didn't. You have seven days or something like that.

Emily started to weep, and Colleen pulled her into a comforting embrace.

Emily: His name is Daniel Hungblegger.

Meeting Hungblegger

Colleen, Emily, and Celly sat in a car outside Daniel's home. Cellrod dashed out of the car to his dad's door, with Emily following closely behind, while Colleen observed.

Cellrod knocked twice, and a young man answered the door, slightly older than Cellrod.

Young Man: Hello?

Emily: Is Danny there?

Young Man: Who are you?

Emily: A friend of Danny's. My name is Emily Kokotan.

The young man called for Daniel, referring to him as "dad." Cellrod's eyes widened as he realized the young man was his brother. Daniel, a tall, bald man, appeared at the door, the young man standing in the doorway.

Daniel: Emily?

Cellrod gasped and teared up.

Daniel: What's going on? Are you okay?

Emily: Can we talk alone?

Daniel: Hanga, let me be, good son.

Hanga, the young man, left for the kitchen, and Daniel shut the door.

Daniel: What's this about?

Emily: This (gesturing to her son) is Celly. He is your son, your firstborn.

Daniel looked over at Cellrod, covering his mouth.

Cellrod: Hi, hi Dad. I like your vest.

Daniel looked back at Emily.

Daniel: How old is he, 16?

Emily: The frat house party was 15 years ago. This is your son. A boy needs his dad.

Daniel: So, you came to my house? My wife is dying... My family would never forgive me.

Cellrod: We can meet in secret.

Daniel appeared deep in thought. He proposed the idea of telling his family that his late brother Isaac would be Celly's father, allowing him to still be part of the family.

Gabriel's First Mission

After three weeks of army training, Gabriel received his first mission: to invade an Ash island and eliminate as many subjects as possible.

Gabriel's Team:

- Patrick Cojeds
- Jim Lanka
- Alex Boland
- Egan Komov
- Renman Hovk the 3rd

The team, along with others, was dropped off in the Oka jungles. As they reached a small village, Gabriel noticed children playing and felt sick. Jim noticed Gabriel trembling with the gun in his hand.

Jim: You okay, Gabe?

Everyone turned to Gabriel, who swallowed hard, then their team leader, Patrick, approached him.

Patrick: Not getting weak there, now, clone?

Gabriel: Are we going to kill those kids too?

Patrick chuckled.

Patrick: They said everyone on this island. We take it, we win.

Patrick and the team rushed out of the trees into the village, initiating a massacre of the Ash people. Gabriel stood motionless until a woman with an axe charged at him, and he put her down. Following Patrick's lead, Gabriel began to kill. Two hours later, West Oka was taken by Spinlenia, with over a thousand killed. Gabriel stepped around the dead children, feeling ashamed and guilty, as Jim and Egan approached him, patting him on the back.

Egan: Good job clone!

Gabriel: Sure.

Jim: we had no choice Gabriel let's finish burning the island.

Gabriel set huts and houses on fire in one house he goes in and sees a little girl under the table looking up at him with big green eyes. Gabriel Jose out his hand in the girl maybe age 6 take his hair and Gabriel quietly runs her to the back of the Woods. He tells her to run, and she does.

She did look back at him but kept going as fast as she could. Gabriel and his team wait to hear worse than 4 hours later a helicopter lands and picks them Up.

Act seven

Gabriel is crying in his dorm bathroom he has the shower going so nobody can hear him.

They meet in the visiting rooms.

Lisa: You are granted a 12-hour visit.

Colleen: Really? That's so long.

Lisa: It's a sex meeting, you need to let off steam.

Colleen: Oh.

Gabriel blush and looks away then he and his wife are giving a cabin on base. Colleen begins to cook she is cooking roast beef and beans. She walks over to the couch where Gabriel is sitting watching TV. She said next to him if she wraps her arm around him and he looks her in her eyes and smile.

Colleen: So, a sex meeting huh?

Colleen giggles.

Gabriel: I guess so. Yea.

Colleen: I recall when we first made love it was finals week in college, we went on our first ice cream date then you took me to your dorm we made passionate love. You were so sweet and gentle seem like forever ago.

Gabriel frowns.

Gabriel: I wish I could remember it seems nice.

Colleen frowns.

Colleen: yeah, have they introduced you to music yet?

Gabriel's eyes widen.

Gabriel: What is music?

Colleen takes out a speaker and puts in Nirvana's spank thru and Colleen does a goofy Rock and roll dance,

Gabriel smile as he gets the urge dance to, he emerged from the couch. And dances with his wife they grab each other's hands laughing.

Gabriel: it’s pleasing to my ears!

Colleen: that's Mr. Cobain you will get to know more of him and teach his music to our kiddos.

Gabriel bangs his head with a smile from ear-to-ear. Gabriel: How is the baby?

Colleen: They're fine recent I went to the doctor the other day together.

Gabriel put his hands on his hips.

Gabriel: Boy or girl?

Colleen: I don't want to know that it be a surprise.

Gabriel smiles.

Gabriel: I'm excited to be a dad, Colleen. I really am.

Colleen places her hand on his face and pulled him close.

They kiss for a moment then it got heavy. Colleen got up on laid on the bed.

They giggle.

Gabriel kisses her belly then he pulls off his shirt.

Colleen is feeling a bit nervous she felt like she was being unfaithful in a way to the old Gabriel.

Colleen: What do you have in mind?

Gabriel: Undress…. slow.

She does and he can feel himself getting hard. Colleen exposes her chest just as. He pulls down his pants and she storks him gently.

Gabriel: Oh Colleen. He said in her ear as she jerks him off.

At war

Gabriel has 20 POWs change walking them to their death as Jim dug their graves.

Ash boy: You will lose this war!

Patrick: why you say that shit face?

Ash boy: We have more men than you have. We will get our princess back and we will rape your wives and daughters.

Patrick puts out his cigar on the boy's face. Patrick bends the boy soldier over a truck. Laughing Patrick pulls down the young shoulder's pants. Patrick starts to unbuckle his belt.

Gabriel: What are you doing?

Patrick: Raping him till he bleeds.

Patrick rapes the boy who was maybe round the age of 19. The boy tried to fight back but Patrick was bigger and stronger. Back at the base, Gabriel sat in the lobby, his eyes fixed on the war unfolding on the news. Lundy's decision to join the fight alongside Dorshka aiding Spinlenia added a new layer of complexity. Gabriel rose to call his wife, but was abruptly informed he could no longer make phone calls. Perplexed, he sought out Jim and borrowed his phone, only for Reese to pick up.

Reese: What's up, Brother?

Gabriel: Hi, Reese. Where's Colleen?

Reese: She stepped out. Are you okay?

Gabriel: They won't let me call her. I'm using a buddy's phone.

Reese: Did they say why?

Gabriel: No, they didn't. Just tell her to try calling me and see if they'll let her through.

Reese: Alright, hang in there, little bro.

Gabriel waited for four agonizing hours with no word from Colleen, prompting him to use Jim's phone again.

Gabriel: Colleen?

Colleen: What do you mean they won't let you call me? What about visiting?

Reese worriedly bit his nails in the background.

Gabriel: They said too much contact with a woman could weaken me for war.

Colleen said nothing, her eyes brimming with tears as panic began to grip her.

Colleen: Motherfuckers!

Gabriel: I can't stay here! I can't lose you, or Reese, or the baby. They lied!

Colleen: We'll figure something out. Stay calm, my love.

Later, Gabriel approached Lisa in her office, finding her typing away.

Gabriel: I think I've been a good soldier, Lisa...

Lisa: You have been.

Gabriel: But seeing Colleen is not making me weak.

Lisa stopped typing, crossed her arms and legs, and turned to face him.

Lisa: Hesitation in war, Gabriel, it'll get you killed. We can't afford any vulnerabilities.

Gabriel: I'm not a monster.

Lisa: But the Ash Lundys are! If we want to win, we have to be just like them.

Gabriel: I killed a guy for Spinlenia on my first day. That's not weak.

Lisa: What do you want, Gabriel?

Gabriel: Two things. I want a week with my family, and I want my memories back.

Lisa glanced away briefly before meeting his gaze again, standing and approaching Gabriel with her hands on her hips.

Lisa: No, Gabriel.

Gabriel flushed with frustration and frowned.

Gabriel: Then let me be with my family.

Lisa: I have work to do. Serve your country. Soon the war will be over, okay?

That night, at 4:38 am, April was awakened by Jim, who covered Gabriel's mouth and offered him a pill. Jim whispered that it was a way out of the war, a sleeper pill that would make him appear lifeless for eight hours. Confused but desperate, Gabriel took the pill and quickly passed out.

When he regained consciousness, he found himself in a car with his wife, his brother Reese driving, Emily, and her son.

Reese stopped the car abruptly, alarmed by Gabriel's bloody chest, caused by the removal of his tracking device when they thought he was dead.

Reese: Gabe! Are you okay?

Gabriel: What? Who are these people? (Looking at Emily's son and her too)

Emily chuckled.

Colleen: They're your friends. They're going to help us get to Cobed, then Check, and hopefully Dossell Court.

Gabriel turned to Emily and her son.

Cellrod: You look just like him.

Emily: He is him. He's Gabriel Lilas.

Gabriel's eyes widened as his brother started the car and drove off. He sank back into the seat.

Gabriel: Do you have my memories?

Reese: Your spy buddy is going to break into their system and get them for us.

Gabriel: Jim?

Colleen: Yes.

Gabriel: Okay.

Emily checked the GPS on her wrist.

Emily: We're an hour away. We'll be there soonish.

Reese: We're going to a blind spot on the border at night, ditch the car, and cross over.

Gabriel: Can't we do it legally?

Colleen: You're supposed to be dead, honey. We can't risk your dead status.

Gabriel: Then walking it is.

Colleen kissed Gabriel on the head.

As night fell over Cobad's Blindspot, Zekomed, Emily, Cellrod, Colleen, Reese, and Gabriel abandoned their car and set it ablaze, avoiding the arduous Long Walk to the hotel, a 28-minute trek away. Instead, they crossed the border and booked a room. Gabriel, concealing his distinctive hair color beneath a hoodie, received a beer from his brother.

Gabriel: Thanks, Reese.

Reese: Have you thought of any baby names yet?

Gabriel: Not really... Wait, actually, there's one I like. Ansel sounds pretty cool for a boy.

Reese: Ansel Lilas? Rolls off the tongue well. What about for a girl?

Gabriel: Lilliam.

Reese: Beautiful names. You should tell your lady.

Gabriel nodded, cracked open the beer, and began to drink as he chatted with Reese while Emily and Colleen conversed nearby. Colleen expressed her fears to Emily, worrying that the government would find and harm them for deceiving them. Emily reassured her, asserting that they were not under suspicion and would be safe once they reached Dossell Court.

That night, Colleen received a phone call from Jim, who informed her that he was having trouble locating Gabriel's memories but was making progress. Colleen thanked him, then climbed into bed with a sleeping Gabriel, cuddling him close.

Gabriel was the first to wake up to a loud beeping sound from the TV. Rushing to investigate, he discovered his own image alongside Reese and Colleen's, labeled as fugitives who had lost their citizenship for stealing government property. Panic ensued among the group, except for Cellrod.

Cellrod: Calm down. We just need to change our appearances.

Emily suggested dyeing Gabriel's hair first, as he was not pictured on the news. She left with her son to purchase different hair dyes, returning to the hotel to begin the transformation. Gabriel received a dark brown dye, masking his purplish-blue hair, while Colleen opted for blonde hair and a short cut. Reese's beard was shaved off, his hair dyed red, and they consulted a map to plan their route to Dossell Court.

Colleen: We need to call Jim.

Emily: I'm afraid he might be dead.

Colleen: How do you know?

Emily: He hasn't contacted us, and now we're all over the news.

Reese made the call, and after several rings, Jim answered, sounding out of breath.

Jim: Gabe's people?

Reese: Yes! Are you okay?

Jim: No! They're after me. I'm running for my life to my friend's house. I've got Gabe's memories. Meet me in Dossell Court, at Somood Cave!

Reese: We're not far. Where in Dossell?

Jim: Got to go. Meet in the cave!

With that, Jim hung up, restarted the car, and headed for the desert near Chec.

Cellrod turned to Gabriel.

Cellrod: I met my father.

Gabriel: You didn't know him?

Cellrod: Not for most of my life. He accepted me but pretended to be my uncle. I'm okay with it, though.

Gabriel: At least he didn't reject you outright.

Cellrod: That's all that matters. A boy needs his father. So, about your son... What will you call him?

Gabriel: We're not sure of the gender yet.

Colleen playfully smacked Cellrod on the head, and they all laughed.

Gabriel: We're having a boy.

Cellrod: That's right.

Colleen: You silly boy. Yes, Gabe. It's a boy in my belly.

Gabriel: How about the name Ansel?

Colleen: Ansel? I love it. That's settled then.

Cellrod: I could be Uncle Celly.

Colleen: Or God-dad.

Cellrod: Love that. Love you guys so much.

Gabriel pulled Colleen and Cellrod into a warm embrace.

Gabriel: I love you guys!

Suddenly, Reese slammed on the brakes.

Reese: Fuck!

Emily: What's wrong?

Reese: Police.

The police approached, shining a light into the car.

Police Woman: You are comans.

Reese: No, we're Vice, on a family road trip.

Police Woman: Show us your papers.

Reese: (Worried) Okay.

Reese reached for his gun, pointing it at the officers and killing them. Panic erupted in the car, and Reese sped away, leaving the dead officers by the roadside.

Colleen: Fuck, Reese!

Reese: They would have arrested us. I had to protect us. I'm sorry I killed them. So what?

Emily: We need to get to Dossell fast!

Reese: I know.

Arriving at Dossell Court Cave, Gabriel received a text from Jim to meet him inside. As they navigated the cave, they heard a ticking sound. Investigating with flashlights, they found nothing.

Gabriel: We need to keep moving. We're almost there.

Reese: Gabe's right. The ticking noise is irrelevant.

Suddenly, a blinding light and a deafening bang sent them flying. Gabriel screamed; his eyes squeezed shut. When he opened them, he found himself at the age of 23, moving into a new apartment. Across the way, he saw Colleen struggling with her bags, and his heart skipped a beat. Boom!!!

Gabriel kisses colleen for the first time, he watches as she gets into the bed. He kisses the back of her neck as he is on top of her.

Present

Gabriel opens his silver eyes in darkness with a major headache and pain in the midst of all that he knew who he was now.

Made in the USA
Columbia, SC
18 June 2024

37258623R00075